THE TROLL
WITH NO HEART
IN HIS BODY

Other Books Illustrated by Betsy Bowen
Published by the University of Minnesota Press

Big Belching Bog by Phyllis Root
Great Wolf and the Good Woodsman by Helen Hoover
Twelve Owls by Laura Erickson
Hawk Ridge: Minnesota's Birds of Prey by Laura Erickson

THE TROLL WITH NO HEART IN HIS BODY

and Other Tales of Trolls from Norway

retold by LISE LUNGE-LARSEN

woodcuts by BETSY BOWEN

UNIVERSITY OF MINNESOTA PRESS

MINNEAPOLIS
LONDON

To the memory of my mother and father,
and to my tante Mari: takk for all hjelpen
—L. L.-L.

To Ernest Harvey Olsen, my father,
who gave me the first taste of my Scandinavian heritage
—B. B.

The University of Minnesota Press gratefully acknowledges assistance provided for the publication of this volume by the John K. and Elsie Lampert Fesler Fund.

Originally published in 1999 by Houghton Mifflin Company

First University of Minnesota Press edition, 2013. Reprinted by special arrangement with Houghton Mifflin Harcourt Publishing Company.

Published by the University of Minnesota Press
111 Third Avenue South, Suite 290
Minneapolis, MN 55401-2520
http://www.upress.umn.edu

Library of Congress Cataloging-in-Publication Data
The troll with no heart in his body and other tales of trolls from Norway /
retold by Lise Lunge-Larsen ; woodcuts by Betsy Bowen.
Folktales mainly from Peter Christian Asbjørnsen and Jørgen Moe's collection *Samlede eventyr.*
Includes bibliographical references.
ISBN 978-0-8166-8457-1
1. Trolls — Folklore. 2. Folklore — Norway. I. Bowen, Betsy, ill. II. Asbjørnsen, Peter Christian,
1812–1885. *Samlede eventyr.* English. III. Moe, Jørgen Engebretsen, 1813–1882. IV. Title.
PZ8.1.L9735Tr   1999
398.2'09481'01 — dc21   98-43244

Printed in China on acid-free paper

The University of Minnesota is an equal-opportunity educator and employer.

20 19 18 17 16 15 14 13   10 9 8 7 6 5 4 3 2 1

CONTENTS

A Note from the Author

TROLLS! WHEN I WAS A CHILD GROWING UP IN NORWAY, JUST THE mention of that word sent chills down my spine. Trolls were everywhere: in the mountains, in the forests, certainly under bridges, and even in our house. One of my favorite memories is of my father, pillows stuffed under his shirt to enlarge his towering 6-foot-3-inch frame, storming into our bedroom at night roaring, *"I smell the smell of human flesh!"* Trolls were even in the words we used. When I was bad my mother called me *"en trollunge,"* a troll child. And, of course, trolls were in the stories—the stories I adored and always begged for. Now, having been a storyteller for more than twenty years, I find American children also begging for "just one more troll story." What *are* trolls and why do children love them so much?

Trolls are giants shaped by the ancient Norse mythology and by the towering Scandinavian landscape. Long before there were people, there were trolls. According to Norse mythology, the first thing in the world was a huge, wild frost giant named Ymir (ee-meer). From his feet sprouted the race of the trolls. The first troll had six heads and six arms and quickly grew to a monstrous size. Ever since, Norway has been inhabited by these giants.

Clearly, one aspect of children's fascination with trolls is that they make the very landscape come alive. Not only are trolls *of* the landscape, they also return *to* and shape the landscape around them when they die. One of my most vivid childhood memories is of walking in the woods with my mother when I was about three. We ambled along the trail in the dark old-growth forest filled with filtered sunlight, when my mother suddenly grabbed my arm and whispered, "Look! There's a troll."

I actually thought my last moment had come, until I saw where she pointed: to a dead troll that had turned into an overturned tree root. Together we examined the troll, found his nose, arms, and even his eye sockets. It was a magical moment, and to this day I point out all the dead trolls in the landscape to my children and their friends: A huge rock pile is a troll that burst, a tree root lying on its side is an ancient troll, an oddly shaped rock may be part of a nose. Last summer my eight-year-old son, swimming in Lake Superior, spotted an unusually round white rock. He dove for it and proudly emerged with a "troll's eyeball."

But perhaps the greatest reason children love troll stories is because children *need* stories like them. Nothing can truly show children, even adults, more about how to live, about who they are, and about their place in the world, and the struggles of life than a good folktale, and these troll stories I count among the best. Yet today many children have never heard *any* of the great folktales, including troll stories.

As a society we have come to think of folktales as amusing entertainment, quaint relics of the past. We certainly do not view them as vehicles for understanding. Yet folktales explore issues as complex as the nature of good and evil, and the triumph of kindness and patience over bullying and anger. Folktales reveal universal truths. Take the story of "Butterball," a perennial favorite in my storytelling sessions. In this story a troll hag, carrying her head under her armpit, captures a silly, butter-loving boy because he ignores his mother's advice. The troll hag orders her daughter to cook stew out of Butterball while she fetches her husband, the

7

troll. In the end this seemingly silly boy outwits the daughter and gets rid of the entire troll pack. This story is the most frequently requested story in my repertoire. I had always thought its principal attraction was the hideous troll herself, who carried her head under her armpit, until one a day a child blurted out, "How come Butterball is so stupid while he is at home with his mom, but when he is on his own he manages just fine?" After years of telling this story the compelling element, immediately spotted by a child, had completely escaped me: your family, your community can help, but ultimately you have what you need to succeed inside yourself. Strength comes from within.

Because they speak to our *inner* circumstances, great folktales speak to all children, regardless of age, race, gender, and outer circumstances. Recently I told troll stories to a group of children, ages three through thirteen. Despite the disparity in ages, the children sat equally spellbound as story after story unfolded. I was reminded of what a psychologist had told me about children's fascination with trolls and with folktales in general. He believes these stories bypass later brain development and go directly to the ancient part of the brain, where they reside right next to fire. What a lovely image and how appropriate! The way children sit around a fire, the way they are warmed by it, is exactly the way they sit when listening to a good story. Like fire, a good story is slightly dangerous, spellbinding, and warming.

Fire, anthropologists tell us, is one of the elements that separate humans from animals. Basically, four main practices make us human:

- Using fire.
- Creating and using complex tools, including writing.

- Tilling the soil.
- Engaging in ritual and ceremony, including storytelling.

This means that love of story is part of what makes us human; it is innate, and it helps us to survive. We need fire, and we need to hunt, to gather, to fashion clothes, and to till the soil for our physical survival. While ritual and storytelling now may seem unnecessary for the survival of the body, they are necessary for the survival of the soul.

Think of the lives of so many children today. Do they get much of what helps their soul and humanity survive? Do they sit around campfires, have candlelit dinners? Can they garden? Do they learn to draw, to whittle, to knit, to weave, to sew, to fashion things of clay? Do they hear great stories? Many children receive so little of what nourishes their soul that it seems as though they turn from a positive expression of their humanity to a destructive one: They grasp fire, but it becomes arson; they want to use tools, but the tools become guns; they want to till the soil, but their world is paved over, so they ransack and destroy; and there is less and less ritual or structure in their family life, so they seek the ritual and structure of gangs. Such children are clearly grasping for their humanity, but it seems we do not know how to help them find it.

Telling or reading folktales is one way to cultivate a child's soul and humanity. With their ancient symbolic images, such stories reach deep inside children to connect them with their essential nature. Troll stories do this better than many folktales because the troll acts as such a clear foil to the hero or heroine. Everything about the troll is contradictory to human nature: They are enormous, grotesque

creatures with superhuman strength. They are full of treachery and falseness and stand for all that is base and evil. To fight trolls, you can't be like them or use their weapons. Thus, battling trolls brings out the very best in those who dare confront them: intelligence and ingenuity, courage and persistence, kindness and pluck, and the ability of men and women to rely on what each has to offer. To do battle with a troll is to learn to draw on the best of our humanity.

Children's feelings are never misplaced in troll stories, and they soon learn to trust them. Here right and wrong are kept steadily in sight. In a world where children are confused by a myriad of opposing and shifting values, these stories serve as a rudder. They teach eternal truths about how to live that will never become irrelevant.

Here are fifteen of the most basic lessons I have found repeated over twenty years as a storyteller:

- Remember who you are.
- Be true to your own nature.
- Follow your dreams.
- Every action has consequences, so be attentive, be kind, and always do what is right.
- Life is a journey; nobody else can do that journey for you.
- Your journey will unfold according to a pattern. The pattern is a guide.
- Use your gifts.
- Help will be offered when you most need it and least expect it.
- Despite the odds, good will triumph over evil, love over hatred.

- Don't ever give up.
- Be careful in what you wish for.
- Things are not always as they appear.
- Everything you need can be found inside yourself; it is always there.
- Miracles happen.
- There is magic in the world.

Over and over again, in wonderful, fanciful stories, these themes are repeated in a predictable formula that exactly mirrors the child's view of the world. Children, like the heroes and heroines in these stories, perceive their lives to be constantly threatened. Will I lose a tooth? Will I be invited to play? Will I learn to read? By living a life immersed in great stories and themes, children will see that they have the resources needed to solve life's struggles. And, while listening to these stories, children can rest for a while in a world that mirrors their own, full of magic and the possibility of greatness that lies within the human heart.

So light a candle, or better yet, light the fire, gather the children, and enjoy the spell of the trolls.

THE NORWEGIAN LANDSCAPE is alive with trolls.
Not only are trolls of the landscape, they return to
and shape the landscape around them when they die.

NORTH
• POLE

CANADA

GREENLAND

RUSSIA

NORWAY

ICELAND

O F

N I A

THE STORIES

MANY PEOPLE THINK TROLLS ARE LIKE GNOMES: TINY CHUBBY people wearing red pointed caps. Others think trolls are little plastic toys with pink or orange hair. Norwegian trolls, which are the first trolls, aren't like that at all. They're giants. They can be so big that their heads loom above the tallest treetops. In fact, they are so big that they have to live inside mountains or under really tall bridges.

Trolls are ugly to look at. Their eyes can be the size of potlids, and their noses as long as rake handles. Not only that, trolls love to eat children or little animals. Fortunately, the brain inside that huge head is tiny. Even a little goat can figure out how to outsmart a troll.

The Three Billy Goats Gruff

ONCE UPON A TIME, a long long time ago, way up in the mountains of Norway, there lived three goats and the names of all three were The Billy Goats Gruff. Now these goats needed to go up into the mountains in the summertime because that's where the grass was greenest. But in order to get there they had to cross an enormous bridge, and underneath that bridge lived a huge hideous troll. His eyes were as big as pewter plates and his nose as long as a poker. But there was no way around it. Across the bridge they had to go.

The first one to cross the bridge was the teeniest tiniest of the three billy goats. When he walked across the bridge it made a little sound like this:

Tripp, trap

Tripp, trap

"WHO'S THAT STEPPING ON MY BRIDGE?" roared the troll.

"Oh, it's only me. I'm the teeniest, tiniest of the Three Billy Goats Gruff and I'm on my way up into the mountains to get fat," whispered the little goat in his little goat voice.

"WELL, I'M COMING TO GOBBLE YOU UP NOW," roared the troll.

"Oh, please don't eat me up. If you wait a little longer my brother will come and he is much bigger and fatter than I am."

"OH, ALL RIGHT THEN," huffed the troll. And the little goat ran away as fast as he could.

The next one to cross the bridge was the second of the three billy goats, and when he walked across the bridge it made a sound like this:

TRIPP, TRAPP

TRIPP, TRAPP

"WHO'S THAT STEPPING ACROSS MY BRIDGE?" shouted the troll.

"It's mmm . . . me, the sss . . . second of the Three BBBB . . . Billy Goats GG . . . Gruff and I'm on mmm . . . my way to the mountains to get fat," stammered the goat in a shaking voice.

"WELL, I'M COMING TO GOBBLE YOU UP NOW," bellowed the troll.

"Oh, ppp . . . please don't eat me up. Why don't you wait a little while till my bbb . . . brother comes. He's much bigger and fatter . . . and tastier too."

"ALL RIGHT THEN," roared the troll and the little goat ran across the bridge as fast as his little legs would go.

Now the next one to walk across the bridge was the biggest of the three billy goats. His fur was shimmering and shining and on his head were two gigantic horns. He was so heavy that when he walked across the bridge it sounded like thunder:

TRIPP, TRAPP

TRIPP, TRAPP

"WHO'S THAT STEPPING ON MY BRIDGE?" roared the troll, for now he was really hungry.

"It's **ME**. I'm the biggest of The Three Billy Goats Gruff and I'm on my way up into the mountains to get fat," boomed the goat in his deep voice.

"WELL, I'M COMING TO GOBBLE YOU UP NOW."

"Why don't you come along," the goat taunted.

"I've got two spears,

With those I'll poke out your eyeballs and your ears.

I've got hooves as strong as stones,

With those I'll break your body and your bones."

And he went at the troll and broke every bone in his body and poked his eyes out and sent him way down into the river. Then he went with his brothers up into the mountains, where they ate and got so big and so fat, that if the fat hasn't fallen off them yet, why, they're still there.

Snipp, snapp, snute (snip, snup, snoo-TA)

Her er eventyret ute! (haer aer ayvan-TEER-a ooTA)

Snip, snap, snout,
This tale's told out!

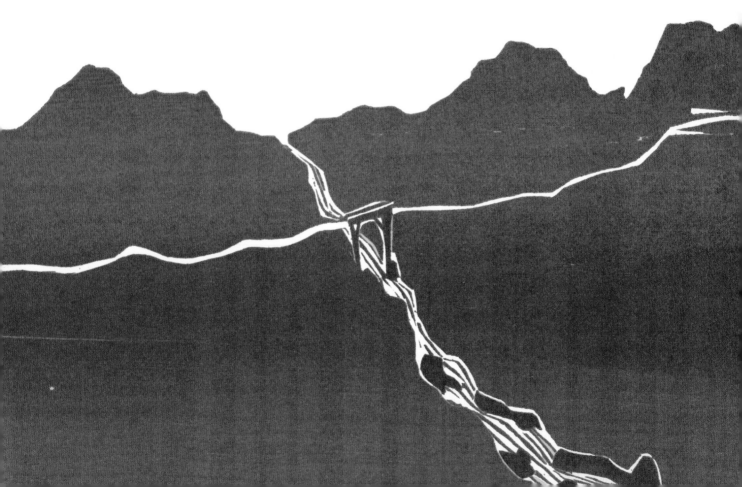

This story is from Asbjørnsen and Moe, "De Tre Bukkene Bruse Som gikk til Seters For å Gjøre seg Fete." This is the best known Norwegian folktale. In fact, I believe that in the 1950s it was voted the most popular story among American children. Frequently, when speaking with adults about trolls, they say, "Well I know they live under bridges." My version is substantially like the Norwegian version. There is not much one can do to improve a story as good as this one. It is the first story I told in English.

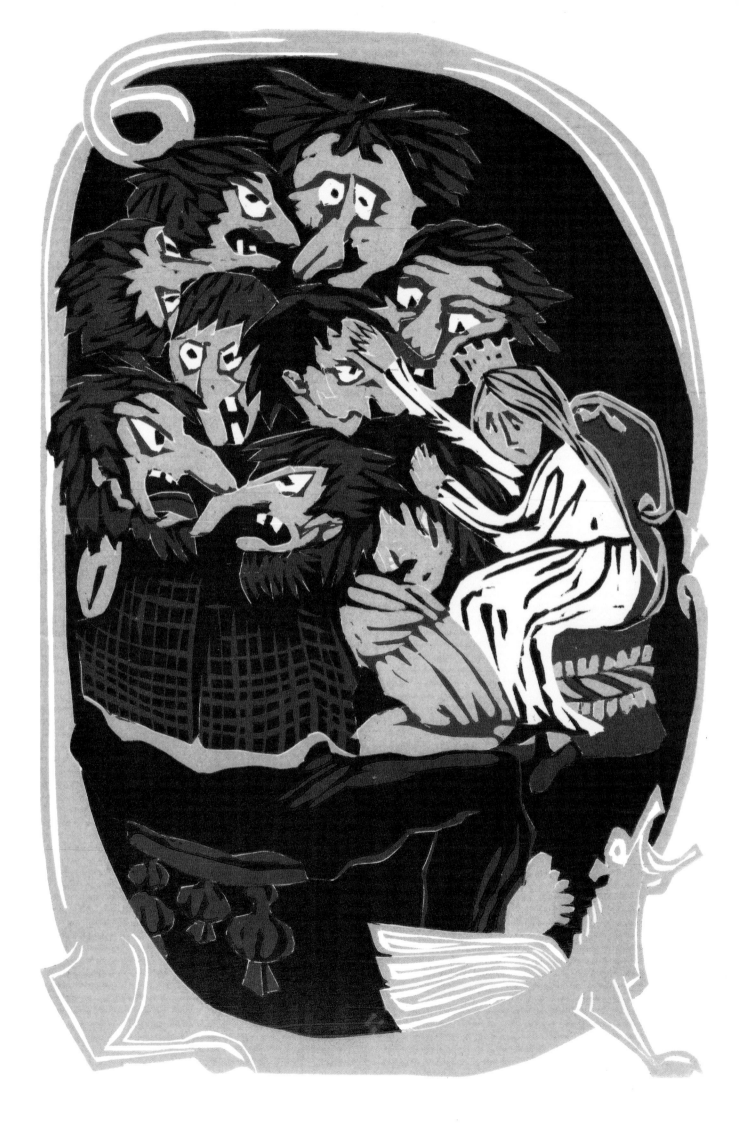

ALL TROLLS ARE UGLY, BUT THE UGLIEST OF ALL ARE THE TROLLS with three, six, or nine heads. They get terrible headaches, probably from the different heads arguing with each other, and the only thing that can soothe them is being gently rubbed by the hands of a princess. That's why trolls often steal princesses and keep them captive inside their mountain homes. To figure out how to get rescued from a troll, you have to know their greatest weakness. Trolls, you see, think they are very smart, and they love to brag about how clever they are. The prince and princess in this story know that if they can make the trolls boast, they may give away important clues. They also know that if the sun shines directly on a troll, he will burst and turn to stone.

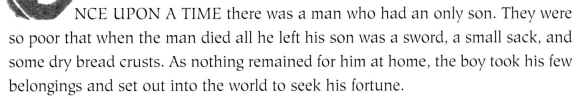

The Boy Who Became a Lion, a Falcon, and an Ant

ONCE UPON A TIME there was a man who had an only son. They were so poor that when the man died all he left his son was a sword, a small sack, and some dry bread crusts. As nothing remained for him at home, the boy took his few belongings and set out into the world to seek his fortune.

His way lay across a mountain, and when he had climbed high enough to get a view of his surroundings, he spotted a lion, a falcon, and an ant quarreling over a dead horse. The boy was frightened at the sight of the lion and wanted to hide. The lion saw him, however, and called for him to come and settle their quarrel. The boy went over and took a good look. Then he pulled out his sword and divided the horse as best he could.

To the lion he gave the large joints, saying, "The lion should have the most, for he is the biggest and strongest." Then he gave the liver and the tasty tidbits to the falcon. "The falcon should have the tastiest bits, for he is such a dainty eater." Last he gave the head to the ant, "For he likes creeping in nooks and crannies," he said.

The three animals were so pleased with the clever way the boy had divided

the horse that they wanted to reward him. But the boy just smiled. "If I have helped you, that is reward enough for me."

Still the animals insisted. "If there is nothing else you want, perhaps you would like three wishes?" the lion finally said. The boy liked that idea, but he could not think of what to wish for.

"Would you like to be able to turn into a lion?" asked the lion.

"And a falcon?" said the falcon.

"And an ant?" added the ant.

The boy thought this might be useful so he made the wishes.

Immediately, he threw away his sword and sack and turned himself into a falcon. He bristled his new wings, test them on the wind a few times, and took off. He flew over mountains and valleys and forests. As he flew over a large lake his wings became so sore he could hardly fly on. At last he spotted a huge rocky crag in the lake and landed there. It was an odd-looking rock, jagged and rough and with a large outcropping on one side. Being curious, he changed himself into an ant and spent some time exploring it.

After he had rested he became a falcon again and flew all the way to the king's farm. There he landed on a branch outside the princess's window. When she saw the bird she thought it so beautiful that she wanted to keep it. She coaxed it to her and as soon as the bird was in her room, she slammed the window shut, and locked it in a cage.

But the boy was not worried. When night came, he just turned himself into an ant and crawled out of the cage. Then he became a boy again and went and sat down by the sleeping princess. She awoke and screamed with fright, but the boy calmed her.

"Why do you scream so? I'm not going to hurt you."

"I thought you were the troll I have been promised to."

"How in the world did you get promised to a troll?" asked the boy.

"Two other trolls have already stolen my sisters," said the princess, "and now a horrible monster with nine heads wants me for his bride or he will destroy my father's kingdom. Every Thursday the troll sends his messenger, a dragon with nine heads. My father has managed to hold him off by feeding him pigs, one for each head. Now there are almost no pigs left in the entire kingdom and I am scared to walk outside."

When the boy heard this he was determined to battle the dragon.

The very next morning he went to the king and told him. The king was well pleased, and as it happened to be Thursday the boy immediately set out for the field where the dragon came to receive his pigs.

Soon enough, a huge serpentine shape with enormous webbed wings lashed the air. Its nine heads spouted fiery flames as it swooped down. When there was no sight of its meal it roared and spat, then lifted its enormous body and charged at the boy as if it was going to swallow him alive. In a twinkling the boy became a lion, reared up on his hind legs, and leaped at the dragon, sinking his teeth deep into the scaly body.

The lion tore off one head after another till at last only the ninth head was left. But that was the strongest head. In its mouth were nine forked tongues, and it spouted blazing venom as it lashed its mighty tail and attacked. But the lion was

ready; he jumped nimbly aside, leaped upon the back of the dragon and bit off the last head.

Now the boy went to the king with the good news and the king and princess were overjoyed. The king wanted to reward the boy. But he just smiled and said, "If I have helped you, that is more than enough reward for me." The king insisted there must be something he wanted. Finally the princess leaned over and whispered in her father's ear. With a smile the king turned, saying, "My daughter says if there is nothing else you want, perhaps you would like her for your bride?"

The boy thought that was an excellent idea and so it was settled that he was to marry the princess.

Everyone was happy. Indeed, the boy and the princess were so happy that they forgot about the troll and went walking in the garden to plan their wedding. Suddenly, the horrible troll with nine heads came upon them, seized the princess, and flew off with her through the air.

The boy ran to tell the king, then changed into a falcon and sped off. By now the princess and the troll were out of sight, but the falcon flew in the direction he had seen them go. Soon he came back to the large lake, where he remembered the mysterious rock he had seen during his first flight. He swooped down, changed into an ant, and crept through the crack in the rock.

He crawled farther and farther down until he came to a locked door. But knowing what to do, he just crept through the keyhole. On the other side of the door was a large hall. There he saw a princess rubbing the heads of a troll who had three heads.

"This must be the right way," the boy said to himself, for he realized this was one of the king's older daughters.

He crawled on, and after a while he came to a second locked door. Again he crept through the keyhole. This time he came to a room where another princess sat rubbing the heads of a troll who had six heads. Now he *knew* he was on the right path and hurried on.

Finally he came to a third locked door. On the other side sat the youngest princess with the troll who had nine heads.

He scurried over the floor, crept up her leg, and pinched her. She knew it had to be the boy wanting to speak to her, and asked the big troll permission to go outside. There the boy appeared in his own shape.

"How are we ever going to get you away from here?" he said.

"I don't know," said the princess, "but I will ask the troll some questions. Perhaps he will tell us something useful."

The boy turned back into an ant and settled on her foot. The princess returned to the troll and after a while she began to sigh and appear lost in thought.

"What is all this moaning about?" roared the troll. "You are forgetting to rub my head. The pain is coming back."

"Oh, it's just that I am so sad thinking that perhaps I shall never see my father again," said the princess.

"That's right, you never will," gloated the troll. "You are mine now."

"Is there really no way to see my dear father and my dear country again?"

"There is only one way, but no one will ever discover it," said the troll. "It is a secret."

The princess took the troll's biggest head in her lap and began to rub it. "Perhaps you will tell me? There is no harm in that surely."

The troll thought about this. "No harm, no harm," he said, "for it is impossible to guess and even more impossible to do, even if you knew the secret."

The princess rubbed the head even more. Finally the troll could keep his clever secret no longer. "To free you, someone must find the grain of sand hidden under the ninth tongue in the ninth head of the dragon and drop that grain down the crack in the rock above us. Then and only then would you be free, but nobody will ever guess it," he said, thinking himself very clever indeed.

Well, as soon as the boy heard this he crept down from the princess's foot, out through all the keyholes, and up through the crack in the rock. There he became a falcon and flew to where the dragon lay. He found the ninth head and carefully lifted each tongue. At last he found the tiny grain of sand under the ninth tongue, picked it up with his beak, and flew off. When he came above the rock he took careful aim and dropped the grain of sand so it fell cleanly through the crack.

Suddenly, the rock cracked asunder and the sun shone straight on the three trolls sitting there. With a tremendous explosion the trolls burst and turned to stone. Then the lake dried and turned into lush and beautiful fields and meadows and a golden castle rose up. The three princesses came running out of the castle, and they all returned to the old king's dwelling, where there was no end to the rejoicing.

The boy and the youngest princess were made husband and wife, and there were revels throughout the kingdom for seven whole weeks to celebrate the wedding. Then the boy and the princess went to live in their golden castle and fared well to the end of their days.

Snipp, snapp, snute
Her er eventyret ute!

Snip, snap, snout,
This tale's told out!

From Asbjørnsen and Moe, "Gutten Som Gjorde set til Løve, Falk, og Maur." One English version is in A Time for Trolls: Fairytales From Norway, *translated by Joan Roll-Hansen, Nor-Media, Oslo, 1962. My version is much like the one I learned as a child, with only minor changes to make the telling smoother and easier to follow. The appearance of a lion feels un-Norwegian and suggests that the story originates elsewhere. The trolls, however, are typical with their three, six, and nine heads, their terrifying and covetous manner, and their inability to resist bragging.*

T HE NEXT STORY IS ONE OF MY FAVORITES BECAUSE IT HAS A female troll, called a troll hag, and she doesn't carry her head on top of her shoulders. Instead she carries it underneath her arm. Imagine how scary it would be to hear her deep rumbling voice coming from her armpit! Troll hags are a little different from trolls. They're usually smaller, they can be out in the sun without bursting, and they're quite a bit smarter than the trolls. You have to really use your brain to outwit a troll hag, as this story shows you.

Butterball

O NCE UPON A TIME there was a little boy who lived with his father and mother way up in the mountains of Norway. This boy loved to eat sweet buttery things. Every day when his mother was baking he sat next to her, chatting and eating bits of dough or cookies, and for this reason he had become as round as a ball. So they called him Butterball.

One day the mother was baking and butterball was eating just as usual, when suddenly their dog, Goldtooth, barked loudly. "Butterball, go out and see why Goldtooth is barking so," said the mother. Butterball ran outside. A hideous sight met his eyes. Down from the mountain strode a large troll hag. She carried her head under her left arm, and sticks and root tips protruded from her neck where her head should have been! In her right hand she clutched a large burlap sack.

"Mom, Mom," Butterball wailed. "There's a troll hag coming down the mountain. What shall we do?"

"Quick! Go and hide underneath my baking table. Stay quiet and let me handle everything," said Butterball's mother calmly. "OK," said Butterball and crept underneath the table.

Soon the door shook from loud knocks. "Come in," called Butterball's mother sweetly. The troll hag stooped and squeezed through the doorway.

"Good day. Is Butterball at home today?" rumbled the troll hag from beneath her armpit.

"Oh, I'm so sorry!" said Butterball's mother. "He's out hunting grouse with his father today. It's too bad you missed him."

"Yes, that's too bad," agreed the troll hag, her wicked little eyes darting around the room, "because I have this beautiful little silver knife that I so wanted to give him."

"**Pip, pip**! Here I am," said Butterball and shot out from beneath the table.

"Oh, Butterball, there you are! My back is so sore. Why don't you crawl into the sack and collect the knife yourself?"

Butterball didn't need to be asked twice. He dove into the sack, but no sooner was he inside than the troll hag grabbed the sack, flung it over her shoulder, and rushed out the door.

She had walked for a long time when she finally grew tired and dropped the sack on the road.

"I'm going to take a little nap. Why don't you take one too, and then we'll be on our way," said the troll hag. Soon Butterball heard hacking noises in the forest. The ground shook from the troll hag's snores. Quickly he found the silver knife, sliced a hole in the sack, and escaped. In the forest he found a root about the same size that he was, which he rolled into the sack so it looked as though he was still there. Then he ran home as fast as he could.

The troll hag was fuming with anger when she came home, opened her sack, and discovered the root, so the next day exactly the same thing happened. Butterball and his mother were baking when Goldtooth started barking. Again Butterball ran outside, and again he came right in. "Oh, Mom, that hag is coming back and she's uglier than ever. What shall we do?"

"You know perfectly well what we are going to do. Get under the table, stay still, and don't make a peep, and everything will be all right," replied his mother. Butterball did as his mother told him, and soon there was a loud knock on the door.

"Good day. Is Butterball at home today?" rasped the troll hag's voice from beneath her armpit.

"I'm sorry, but Butterball is out hunting grouse with his father today," said the mother.

"That's too bad," said the hag in her husky voice. "I have this beautiful little silver fork that I so wanted to give to him."

"**Pip, pip!** Here I am," said Butterball, and again he came scooting out from under the table.

"Butterball, my back is still bad. Why don't you crawl into the sack yourself."

He did, and as soon as he was inside, the troll hag grabbed the sack, flung it over her shoulder, and rushed off. Once again the troll hag grew tired and stopped for a nap. As soon as Butterball heard the snores he grabbed the fork and began to

make a hole. It was a little more difficult, but he finally made a small hole. He tore a bigger opening with his fingers and crawled out. This time he found a big round rock to put in the sack in place of himself.

When the troll hag came home she broke her best pot when she dropped the rock into it. Now she was almost trembling with anger.

The third day was just like the others. Goldtooth started to bark and Butterball ran out to see who it was. He came back as fast as his little legs would carry him.

"Mom, oh, mercy me! It's the hag again. What are we to do?"

"Butterball!" said his mother in a stern voice. "You know perfectly well what to do. Crawl under my baking table and stay there. Whatever happens, don't come out and don't make a peep. Now will you promise to listen to me?"

"All right, I'll do just as you say," said Butterball and crawled under the table.

"Good day," said the troll hag's head from beneath the armpit as she squeezed through the door. "Is Butterball at home today?"

"Indeed he is not," said the mother. "He is out in the woods hunting grouse with his father."

"That's too bad," said the hag, "for a I have such a pretty little silver spoon to give him."

"**Pip, pip!** Here I am!" said Butterball and again he jumped out from underneath the table.

"My back is still so stiff, Butterball. You'll have to fetch the spoon for yourself."

Butterball squatted and crept into the sack. No sooner was he inside than the troll hag grabbed the sack, flung it over her shoulders, and strode off. This time she didn't stop until she reached her house. There she called her daughter.

"Now daughter," drooled the troll hag, "you must cook stew out of this juicy Butterball while I'm away fetching your father. When we get back we shall have a feast."

After the troll hag left, the troll daughter wanted to cook Butterball, but she wasn't quite sure how to go about doing it, being neither very clever nor used to cooking. Butterball saw her confusion and said, "I can help you. I know how to cook. I cook with my mom every day."

"Oh, good," said the troll daughter, her mouth already watering at the thought of stew. Butterball explained about pots and pans, fire and water, and finally, the pot and the water were ready.

"Now you have to test the water to see if it is warm enough," said Butterball.

"Huh? How do I do that?" The troll daughter was now so hungry for Butterball stew that slobber ran down her chin.

"Lift the pot lid and plunge your hand into the water."

"How do I know if it is hot?" whined the troll daughter.

"If it burns a little, it's ready," said Butterball.

"Oh, I knew that!" said the troll daughter.

She leaned over the pot and was just about to stick her hand into the water when Butterball bent his head down as if he were a billy goat, took a running start, and butted the troll daughter's behind so hard that into the pot she tipped!

Then he slammed on the lid and ran out of the house and into the forest, where he found the root and the rock and dragged them onto the ledge above the door. He scrambled up after them and waited quietly. In the distance he heard trees being knocked over and rocks being crushed. Soon both the troll and the hag stood in the doorway, their giant noses sniffing the air excitedly.

"Mmm, smells good, Butterball stew," they said.

"Smells good, *daughter* stew," squeaked Butterball, but they paid no attention. They walked into the room.

"Looks good, Butterball stew," said the trolls.

"Looks good, *daughter* stew," peeped Butterball from the ledge.

Then the trolls took to wondering who was making that noise. They walked in the direction of the sound. When they got to the door Butterball threw the root on top of the hag and he threw the rock on top of the troll. They both smashed into thousands of little rocks and Butterball was safe.

Then Butterball went into the mountain, and taking as much gold and silver, diamonds and jewels as he could carry, he went home to his mother. From that time on Butterball and his family lived in the greatest of comfort and safety to the end of their days.

Snipp, snapp, snute
Her er eventyret ute!

Snip, snap, snout,
This tale's told out!

From Asbjørnsen and Moe,
"Smørbukk." In English I have
found this story in Norwegian
Folktales, *translated by Pat Shaw*
Iversen and Carl Norman, Dreyers
Forlag, Oslo, 1978. While this tale is
largely unknown in the United States,
it is enormously popular in Norway. It
was certainly my favorite as a child,
and in twenty years of storytelling it
has proven to be equally popular with
my audiences. There are schools where
the children will not let me leave until
I tell "Butterball." Again my telling is
largely like the story I grew up with. I
have changed the ending slightly, let-
ting Butterball push the troll daughter
into the stew pot, instead of chopping
her head off as the Norwegian text
states. The original ending causes
adults to jump up in protest and seems
too bloody for today's climate. The
toned-down version carries the same
end result and is even more fun to act
out.

SMALL BUSHES AND TREES OFTEN GROW ON TOP OF TROLLS' HEADS. As the trolls get older more shrubs and bushes grow until the trolls themselves begin to look like old trees. The trolls shrink, too, and sometimes become tiny. Some of the meanness goes out of them with age, but they can still be awfully tricky.

Next time you're out for a walk in the woods, look for dead trees, especially overturned tree roots. They might well be trolls that died of old age instead of bursting and becoming stone. Study them carefully and you might spot eye sockets, arms, and a nose (it'll be long). They might look a little like the trolls in this story.

The Handshake

THERE WAS ONCE a man named Haakon (HO-kun) who lost his horse in the mountains. He searched in every crack and crevice, but could not find it. All of a sudden a fog rolled in. It was so thick that Haakon couldn't even see his hand in front of his face. For hours he wandered in the fog until finally he found himself in a pasture.

"I thought there was nothing but rocks and boggy hollows up here," Haakon muttered to himself. Nevertheless, in front of him lay a lush green pasture and at the far end of it, he saw a farm with many buildings. Outside stood an old fellow chopping wood, so Haakon went over to him and asked if he had seen his horse.

"You must ask my father," said the man. "He's sitting by the hearth."

Haakon went inside and there he saw an even older and smaller person cooking bacon over the fire. His whole body was trembling and shaking, and he looked like an old, dry spruce tree all covered with lichen and moss. Again Haakon asked if this fellow had seen the horse, but he replied, "You must ask my father. He's inside the horn you see hanging there on the wall."

Surprised, Haakon looked over at the wall, and there hung a mighty big horn, and inside the horn sat a man who was so old that he could neither see nor walk.

"You're looking for your horse I reckon," squeaked the ancient man. "We had to shut it in the stable for it got into our field. It has suffered no harm. But where are you from?"

"I'm from Seljord," said Haakon.

At that the old man brightened and asked excitedly, "Are folks in Seljord as strong now as they were in the old days? Give me your hand to shake so I can see if you have proper marrow in your fingers."

Haakon reached out to shake the wizened old hand, when the man by the hearth tugged at his sleeve.

"If you want your hand back in one piece, you'd better give him this iron bar instead," he whispered.

"Ha!" shouted the ancient one and squeezed the iron bar so hard that water oozed from it. "There's nothing but sheep's milk in the fingers of folks from Seljord nowadays. It was different in the old days. Haven't you heard of me? I'm called Skaane and I helped St. Olav build the church in Seljord."

"But it's been several hundred years now since St. Olav built that church," said Haakon. "And if you helped him, why are living in this lonely place?"

"When the big bell came to the church I had to move out here. I couldn't stand the sound. I was strong, but St. Olav was stronger than me."

When Haakon was leaving, the old men handed over his horse. Haakon could scarcely recognize it, so fat and sleek had it become. "I told you it suffered no harm," creaked the ancient one. In return for the good treatment Haakon had to promise not to look behind him, but hurry back the same way he had come.

"Good-bye then," said the old man.

"Good-bye yourself," said Haakon and seated himself on the horse. But riding across the pasture he could not resist one last look at the farm. He turned around after all, and the farm was gone! Where the pasture and the farm buildings had stood was the big mountain. It was as black and gray as it had always been, and now Haakon knew that it was trolls he had visited.

Snipp, snapp, snute,
Her er eventyret ute!

> Snip, snap, snout,
> This tale's told out!

This story is based on a tale from Folktales of Norway, *edited by Reidar Christiansen, translated by Pat Shaw Iversen, University of Chicago Press, 1964. It is titled "The Old Troll and the Handshake." The story is a wonderful example of how trolls supposedly helped build a number of churches until St. Olav, the patron saint of Norway, drove them into hiding. There are many local legends on this theme, but this is by far the most interesting one to people outside of Norway. Usually the stories involve trolls turning into stone after their work is done, explaining some of the local, odd rock formations. In this story, the trolls have withdrawn into an elusive world, parallel to, but not easily accessible from ours. Thus we learn that trolls are still among us, but not encountered as readily as in the old days.*

TROLLS ARE NOT ONLY BULLIES, BUT THIEVES TOO. BESIDES TRYING to eat children and goats, they love to steal gold and silver, or better yet, things that are magical. The troll hag in this story is very greedy and sneaky, so it takes the boy some time before he figures out how to use the gifts from the North Wind properly.

The Boy and the North Wind

ONCE UPON A TIME there was a boy named Per who lived with his mother way up in the mountains of Norway. One day Per's mother asked him to fetch flour for bread and cookies. Happily, Per grabbed the biggest bowl he could find and went to the barn. He filled the bowl all the way to the brim and ran back across the yard when suddenly—*whoosh*—the North Wind gusted around the corner and blew all the flour away.

Per returned to the barn, filled the bowl, and hurried back across the yard when—*whoosh*—again the North Wind came and blew the flour away. Once more Per went to the barn. He took all the flour that was left, which wasn't even enough to fill the bowl. He cradled it carefully and hurried across the yard. But—*whoosh*—came the North Wind around the corner and blew all the flour away.

"That means gruel the rest of the winter," scolded Per's mother. "No bread and certainly no cookies until next year."

"What? No bread or cookies? I'm getting the flour back," Per declared and, before his mother could stop him, out the door he went.

All day he trudged through the snow until finally he came to the place where the North Wind lived. "North Wind! You better come out here. I've got to talk to you," Per called, knocking on the door as loudly as he could.

After several minutes the North Wind opened the door. He rubbed his eyes and yawned, "What's all this knocking and hollering about? I can't nap with all this noise around."

"You stole our flour!" Per burst out. "You came to our house three times today

and blew all our flour away, and because of you we won't have any bread all winter. We'll probably starve and it'll be your fault."

The North Wind's face wrinkled up. "Oh, I'm really sorry," he said in his deep booming voice. "Sometimes I get carried away with all my blowing. I don't mean any harm, but there is no way now that I can get the flour back for you." He looked at the boy for a minute. Then he added, "I can't get the flour back, but I can get something else."

He went inside and came back with a cloth. "This cloth is magic. All you have to do is say: 'Cloth, cloth, spread yourself and bring forth wonderful food,' and you will have all the food and drink you'll ever need."

Per thanked the North Wind, took the cloth, and set off. It was almost nighttime. Along the road was an inn where Per decided to spend the night. He knocked at the door and immediately it swung open. Out stepped a troll hag with a nose so long she had tucked it into her belt to keep from tripping.

"Good evening," said the hag in a hoarse voice.

"Good evening," stammered Per. "I was wondering if I could have a bed for tonight?"

"How are you going to pay for it?" rumbled the troll hag.

"I haven't any money, but I could feed you and your guests."

"How?" demanded the troll hag.

Per grabbed each end of the cloth, shook it and said, "Cloth, cloth, spread yourself and bring forth wonderful food."

Instantly the cloth was filled: roasts and chops, meatballs and sausages, vegetables and fruits, pies and puddings, and glorious things to drink.

When all the guests at the inn had their fill, Per rolled up his cloth and went to bed. In the middle of the night, when everyone was sleeping, that troll hag came sneaking up the stairs with a cloth that looked exactly like Per's. She tiptoed into his room and exchanged her cloth for his.

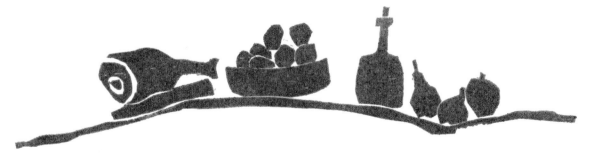

In the morning when Per woke up he grabbed the cloth and ran home. "Mom, Mom, look what the North Wind gave me," he shouted excitedly. Quickly he said the magic words and shook out the cloth. Nothing happened! Again and again he tried, holding the cloth upside down or in different ways, but nothing worked.

"The North Wind has tricked me," Per muttered angrily and stomped off to the North Wind's house before his mom could stop him.

"North Wind! You'd better come out here. I've got to talk to you," Per hollered at the door. After a bit the North Wind came out, rubbing his eyes sleepily.

"You again?" he yawned. "Why are you back so soon?"

"You know why I'm back," Per shouted, almost in tears. "That cloth you gave me, it's no good. It only worked once, and what use is that?"

"Only once? Something is wrong," said the North Wind. "But let's not argue. I'll give you something else." Soon he returned with a ram.

"This is a magic ram. All you have to do is say, 'Ram, ram make money,' and it will make all the money you need."

"Will it work more than once?" Per asked suspiciously.

"Forever," promised the North Wind.

Per took the goat and set off. But it was getting late so he decided to go back to the inn. As soon as he knocked, the troll hag flung open the door. This time soup was dripping from her enormous nose for she'd been using it to stir her pot.

"Good evening. I was wondering if I could have a bed for the night," asked Per.

"How are you going to pay?" growled the hag.

Per turned to the ram and said, "Ram, ram, make money." Instantly, out of its mouth dropped a heap of gold coins. Per paid the hag, spent another coin on food, and then went to bed. In the middle of the night, again the troll hag tiptoed up the stairs, this time with her own ram, which she exchanged for his.

When Per returned home he tried to show his mother what the ram could make. But this ram, if it made anything at all, it surely wasn't money!

Per stormed back to the North Wind, even angrier than before. The North Wind just scratched his big frosty head, shook it, and said, "Something has gone wrong. I'll get one last thing for you, but you'd better use it wisely." He went inside and returned with a stick. This stick is also magic. All you have to do is say, 'Stick, stick, lay on,' and it will beat anyone you want. When you want it to stop, just say, 'Stick, stick, stop beating,' and it will come right back to you."

Per thanked the North Wind and again he went back to the inn.

"Good day," greeted the troll hag.

"Could I have a bed for the night?"

"How do you plan to pay for it?" grunted the troll hag, eyeing the stick. Per fished some leftover coins from his pocket, and this time he went straight to bed.

In the middle of the night, again the hag came sneaking up the stairs. She was sure the stick had some kind of magic. Slowly she tiptoed into the room. Just

as she was about to exchange her stick for his, Per jumped up and yelled, "Stick, stick, lay on."

The stick flew from the pillow and started to beat that troll hag so thoroughly that she hopped from one foot to the other, over chairs and under tables, yowling and yelling, until finally she screamed, "Make it stop, make it stop!"

"Not until you give me back my cloth and my ram," shouted Per.

"I will, I will," screamed the troll hag.

"Stick, stick, stop beating," commanded Per and immediately the stick flew back into his hand. But he kept it safely in his hand as he marched behind the troll hag to fetch his cloth and his ram.

The next day Per returned home with his treasures, and with them he and his mother had all the food and money and protection they needed to the end of their days.

Snipp, snapp, snute
Her er eventyret ute!

Snip, snap, snout,
This tale's told out!

From Asbjørnsen and Moe, "Gutten Som Gikk til Nordenvinden og Krevde Igjen Melet." The version I tell is inspired by my father's vigorous retelling. It has some differences from the original, most notably in the description of the troll hag. In the Norwegian she is not actually a troll hag, but an old crone. My father made her into a troll hag, and I, inspired by a wonderful drawing the Norwegian illustrator Theodore Kittelsen did of a troll hag in the 1800s, added the enormously long nose with stew dripping from it.

TROLLS LOVE TO EAT, BUT THEY ARE USUALLY TOO LAZY TO COOK A good meal for themselves. During the holiday season, with lots of good food, around, they sometimes travel in packs to scare people into giving them food. Then you really get to see what terrible manners trolls have, especially the troll children. They love to fight over the food and they don't even know how to use a knife and a fork! When I had bad manners, my mother called me *en trollunge,* a troll child, to remind me that human nature and manners are far different from the trolls'.

The White Cat in the Dovre Mountain

ONCE UPON A TIME there was a man who caught a big white bear, which he wanted to take as a gift to the king. He happened to cross the Dovre Mountains on Christmas Eve, and there he found a cottage where he asked for shelter for himself and the white bear.

"Heavens no!" exclaimed the farmer, who was named Halvor. "We can't put you up. We can't even stay here ourselves tonight."

"How so?" asked the man with the white bear.

"Every Christmas Eve such a pack of trolls descends on us that we dare not stay. They eat all our food and sleep in our beds and won't leave until every cupboard has been emptied."

"Is that all?" said the man. "I still think you can put me up. My bear can sleep under the stove there and a closet will do for me."

"Suit yourself," said Halvor, "but we're leaving."

Halvor, his wife, and all their children left, and the man and his white bear made themselves comfortable. The house was snug and warm, the tables laden with all the good foods necessary for a feast: sausages and meatballs, fish and chicken, porridge and pie. The man sampled a little of everything, and then he and the white bear settled down for the night.

All at once the air filled with a dreadful stomping, snorting, and screaming as

the troll pack descended on the house. Some were old and some were young, some were big and some were small, some had bushy tails and some had no tails at all, but they all had long, long noses. They fell on the food, ate and drank and fought over the dishes till hardly a crumb was left at all.

The man was awake inside the broom closet and watched everything through a crack in the door. He saw two little trolls fighting over a fat sausage.

"It's mine. I saw it first," screamed one little troll and whapped at the other with his tail.

"No it isn't! I grabbed it before you. It's mine, mine, MINE!" hollered the other little troll even louder and kicked the first troll as hard as he could.

Screaming and tearing at each other, both little trolls pulled at the sausage when, suddenly, it slipped out of their hands and rolled onto the floor, right to the stove where the white bear was sleeping. The man watched as both trolls dropped down and started to search under the tables.

While they were crawling around, one of the trolls spotted the sausage under the stove — and with that he discovered the white bear. He had never seen a white bear, so he thought it was a nice big cat sleeping there under the stove. Chuckling to himself, he grabbed the sausage, pierced a fork through it, heated it on the fire till it glowed, and thrust it under the bear's nose, screaming,

"HERE, PUSSY. DO YOU WANT SOME SAUSAGE?"

The big white bear woke up. With a mighty growl he burst out from under the stove and set upon the troll pack. He snapped at their tails, he clawed at their legs, and chased them around and around the house while they screeched and howled. Finally he chased them all helter-skelter and out of the house. Then he went back to bed.

Next morning, when Halvor and his family returned, they found the man and his bear sound asleep. "If the trolls give you any more trouble, just remind them of the white cat," said the man. "Then they'll trouble you no more, I dare say."

"We'll see," said Halvor.

One year later Halvor was in the forest on the afternoon of Christmas Eve. He was chopping wood for the fire, for he was pretty sure the trolls were coming back again. While he was chopping he suddenly heard a voice calling him from the forest.

"Halvor, Halvor!"

"Yes," answered Halvor.

"Do you still have that big white cat of yours?"

Halvor paused a little, cleared his voice, and hollered back, "Yes, I do. And last summer she had a litter of seven kittens who now are even bigger and angrier than she is."

In the depths of the forest he heard an angry roar, then the troll shouted,

"Well, now you can be sorry, for we will never come back and visit you!"

And the trolls kept their word for since that time they have never come to Christmas dinner at Halvor's little cottage on the Dovre Mountain.

Snipp, snapp, snute
Her er eventyret ute!

Snip, snap, snout,
This tale's told out!

From Asbjørnsen and Moe, "Kjetta på Dovre." The Dovre Mountains in Norway are known for their trolls. The troll king himself, Dovregubben, lived there, and it may have been a host of his many relations who plagued the family in this story.

The Dovre Mountains loom large in Norway's history. Yggdrasil (IG-draa-sill), the world tree of Norse mythology, had its roots deep inside the Dovre Mountains. According to legend, it was the troll king, Dovregubben, who helped Harald Hårfagre (Harald Hairfair) unite Norway and make Harald its first king more than one thousand years ago. These mountains have also inspired much of Norway's best art. The most memorable scenes in Henrik Ibsen's play Peer Gynt *take place there. Edvard Grieg's music,* In the Hall of the Mountain King, *composed for Ibsen's play, is a tribute to the power of the Dovre trolls. Try playing it as you imagine the troll pack descending on Halvor's hut. It'll send chills down your spine.*

WHEN TROLLS WANT SOMETHING REALLY BADLY, THEY MAY PRE-
tend to be nice. Don't ever trust them. The girl in this story is much smarter
than the sailors, who didn't realize that any gift from a troll is dangerous.

P.S. This troll walked all the way from Norway to Greenland. That is so far that
I think some of them walked all the way to America, too.

The Sailors and the Troll

THERE WAS ONCE a troll named Gunnar who was in love with a girl named
Kari. Naturally Kari didn't want to marry a troll, and as she was a clever girl, she
hid in the church whenever she heard his booming footsteps approach. Trolls can't
enter churches; they don't even like the sound of church bells, so Gunnar talked
to Kari from the outside. But no matter how sweetly he spoke, he couldn't get her
to come out. "Never trust a troll," said Kari and settled herself into a pew with her
knitting.

This kept up for many months, but one day Gunnar became so disgusted with
waiting that he hoisted up his pant legs, marched into the sea, and waded all the
way to Greenland.

Some time later, a ship from Kari's town became lost in the storm and ended
up on the shores of Greenland. The sailors were shivering in their cold, wet clothes.
They were hungry, too, for all their food and supplies had washed overboard. As
they huddled around their boat, one of them spotted a light glowing in the mountains. Quickly the sailors set off, hoping to find shelter.

As they got closer, they realized that the light came from a door that opened
into the mountain itself. Now they slowed down. "What if there are trolls living
there?" one asked. "They might kill us and eat us."

"Well, I don't care," replied another. "At least I will die warm instead of freez-
ing to death out here."

That settled it. They went to the mountain and knocked on the door. "Who
dares knock on my door?" bellowed a fierce voice. All at once a large troll flung

open the door. His eyes blazed and he looked ready to strike when one of the sailors shouted, "Gunnar, is that you?" for he recognized the troll who had courted Kari.

Gunnar became so excited to see folks from home that he invited them in for a meal. Happily, the sailors accepted. As they entered the troll's mountain home, their eyes grew wide. The walls were covered in gold and silver and the rooms were filled with amazing treasures. They sat down to eat at a table made of copper. All the dishes were made of silver and the knives and forks of solid gold. Gunnar served them a meal of roasted pork with potatoes and boiled red cabbage. They ate and they ate, and as they ate the troll's food they forgot all caution and happily exchanged news with Gunnar. He was especially eager to hear about Kari.

When the meal was over and dawn was breaking, the troll went farther inside the mountain and returned with two boxes, one blue and one red. First he handed the blue box to the sailors saying, "This is for Kari. Tell her to be sure to try it on as soon as she can, and take care that she does so *outside*. Perhaps she'll be willing to marry me after all. I'll be waiting for her." Then he gave them the red box.

"Now this contains treasures for the church. Give it to the parson and be sure he opens it *inside* the church." The last thing he asked of them was to untie his dog when they returned home, for he had left it chained.

The men took the gifts and promised to let the dog loose. They thanked Gunnar profusely and promised to put in a good word for him with Kari. Then they set sail for Norway.

They sailed for a while, chatting about the great kindness of the troll, when they fell to talking about the gifts. "I wonder what he has sent along. He is certainly a rich fellow," said one. "Yes," said another. "And if we don't take a look now, who knows if we'll ever set our eyes on the treasure." "That's right," added the third sailor. "And if it weren't for us, nobody would get any treasure. I say we take a look. Perhaps he put something in for us too."

They pulled ashore on an island and brought the two boxes with them. First they carefully opened the blue box for Kari. Inside lay the most beautiful belt they had ever seen. It was made of the softest leather and all inlaid with silver and gold

and precious stones. "Ohhh!" gasped the sailors. "I wonder what Kari will say when she sees this?" said the first sailor. "She always said never to trust a troll, but perhaps she'll change her mind," added the second. "We'd best keep it safe. Why don't you tie the belt around that tree there so we don't lose it?" said the third. So the first sailor took the belt and tied it around the tree. As soon as he tied the last knot something very strange happened. The tree started rocking back and forth, back and forth, until it pulled up out of the ground, roots and all, and flew right through the air toward Greenland!

The men were frightened at this, but were still more curious to see what the red box for the church contained. Carefully they lifted the lid and the moment they did, the entire island burst into flames. Screaming, the men leaped into their boat and sailed off in great haste. "Let's not let the dog loose when we come home," said the first sailor. "Who knows what will happen if we do," said the second. "Kari was right," shuddered the third. "Never trust a troll."

They never did again, and don't you either.

Snipp, snapp, snute
Her er eventyret ute!

Snip, snap, snout,
This tale's told out!

This story is based mainly on a tale of Swedish origin, although I consulted both Norwegian and Icelandic stories with similar themes. The Swedish version is in Svenska Folksagnar, edited by Bernt af Klintberg, Bokforlaget PAN/ Norstedts, Stockholm, 1977. The story is titled "Sjømannen och Jatten." For variants used to flesh out this very brief tale, see "The Troll and the Church at Skrea" and "The Ogress Drowned in the Ocean" in Scandinavian Folk Belief and Legend by Reimund Kvideland and Henning Sehmsdorf, University of Minnesota Press, Minneapolis, 1988.

This is the only story featuring a coastal troll. Several variants of this story explain unusual rocks or islands in the ocean between Norway, Iceland, and Greenland. They are trolls caught by early morning sunrays while they were still wading.

YOU HAVE ALREADY LEARNED SOME GOOD WAYS TO TRICK TROLLS, such as making them brag and give away their secrets. The main thing is to stay calm, be brave, and use your head. Trolls are awfully slow thinkers. If you keep remembering how much smarter humans are than trolls, you should be able to outwit even the largest trolls just as the Ashlad does in this story.

The Eating Competition

ONCE UPON A TIME there was a farmer who had three sons. On their farm was a large forest where the farmer often went to cut wood. With the wood he built many wonderful things and provided well for his family.

One day the farmer hurt his back. For weeks he stayed in bed, and after some time the family ran out of money. The farmer tried to get his sons to help, but they were lazy and wouldn't turn their hands to do a thing.

"Oh, Pa," they complained. "You'll be up and about soon. What do you need our help for? We don't like the woods. There are trolls there."

"Trolls," scoffed the farmer. "I knew what to do with them even when I was a little lad. Here you are, nearly grown and still afraid."

The father kept pleading with his sons, and after some time, he finally got them around to his way of thinking. Per, the oldest, was the first one to go. He was a big burly fellow and swaggered off into the woods.

After a bit he came to a spot where some tall, shaggy spruce grew so he rolled up his sleeves, grabbed his ax, and got ready to cut. No sooner had he struck the first blow than out of the forest charged a huge, monstrous troll.

His eyes blazed as he roared, "If you're cutting down my wood I'll kill you and eat you!"

Per got so scared, he just flung his ax aside and took to his heels. When he came home he was panting and sobbing. "You don't know how lucky you are that I am still alive. I met this horrible troll out in the woods and he wanted to kill me and eat me," he wailed.

"What!" exclaimed his father. "You ran away from a troll! Don't you know those creatures are stupid? When I was your age I dealt with trolls all the time. But you, you're behaving like a chicken!"

The next day the second son, Paul, set out, and he fared no better than Per. As soon as he struck the first blow the troll burst out of the forest.

"If you're cutting down my trees, I'll kill you and eat you!" Paul took one look at the troll, tossed his ax aside, and fled as fast as he could. When he got home he was completely out of breath and sobbing like a baby.

"Oh, you don't know how lucky you are that I'm still alive. There was a huge troll out there ready to kill me and eat me."

"Bah," snorted the father. "I can't believe you're scared of a troll. When I was your age, I battled trolls all the time. But you, you're nothing but a chicken."

On the third day the youngest was to set out. He was nicknamed the Ashlad because he spent so much time poking around in the fireplace. When the brothers saw him get ready they burst out laughing.

"What? You go out into the woods? You've hardly been beyond the front door and now you think you're ready to take on a troll?" But the Ashlad paid them no heed. Instead he went to his mother and asked for some provisions. There wasn't much food left, but she gave him a bag of homemade cheese. This he put in a knapsack, picked up his ax, and strode off.

After a bit he, too, came to the place where the large spruce grew and got ready to cut. No sooner had he struck the first blow when out of the woods the troll came screaming and roaring, "If you're cutting down my wood, I'm going to kill you and eat you."

But this boy, he wasn't slow! Quickly he ran to his knapsack, pulled out a large lump of cheese, and squeezed it in his hands until the water squirted. "If you don't watch out," he shouted, "I'm going to squeeze you the way I'm squeezing the water out of this white rock in my hand."

When the troll saw that he got frightened. "Nay, my dear fellow, spare me! I had no idea you were so strong. I'll help you chop," he whimpered.

Well, on that condition the Ashlad agreed to spare him, and the troll was so clever at woodcutting that in a short time they had felled many cords of wood. Evening was drawing near when they finished. All at once the troll looked hungrily at the boy. "How about if you come to my place to have a bite to eat? My place is closer than yours."

The Ashlad said yes and off they went. When they arrived at the mountain where the troll lived, the troll said, "I'll make up the fire. Why don't you get water from the well so we can make porridge?" The boy agreed, but when he went to fetch the water buckets he found they were of solid iron and so huge and heavy that he couldn't so much as budge them. "It's not worth collecting water from these tiny thimbles you have here. I'm going to fetch the entire well, I am!" the Ashlad shouted to the troll.

"Nay, nay, my dear fellow," hollered the troll in dismay. "I can't lose my well. Let's switch tasks. You make the fire and I'll go after the water."

That's what they did, and the troll cooked up a huge pot of porridge. When they were ready to eat, the Ashlad noticed the troll eyeing him hungrily. With a flash in his eyes he suddenly suggested, "If it's all the same to you, let's have an eating competition."

"Oh, yes, yes," the troll hastily agreed. He felt sure he could win at this and then he could have a nice juicy boy for dessert.

Before the Ashlad sat down, he grabbed his knapsack, tied it in front of his stomach, taking care to leave the flap open. They ate and they ate, and after a bit, the Ashlad, instead of putting the food in his mouth, scooped it into the knapsack. When the knapsack was full, he pulled out his knife and ripped a hole in the sack. The troll looked at him but couldn't figure out what was going on, so he kept silent.

Finally the troll put down his spoon and burst out, "I can't manage another mouthful."

"Oh, come on!" said the boy. "I'm barely half full yet. I have room for lots more."

"How do you do that?" wondered the troll.

"Easy," replied the Ashlad. "Do as I did. You take your knife and make a hole in your stomach, then you can eat as much as you wish!"

"But doesn't it hurt?" the troll wanted to know.

"Oh, nothing to speak of," replied the boy.

So the troll did as the boy said. He put his knife to his stomach, and that, as you can imagine, was the end of him. He toppled over and crumbled up into thousands of little rocks. Now that the Ashlad was safe, he went inside the mountain and took all the silver and gold that the troll had stolen and brought it home to his parents. With that, they paid off their debts and lived happily and safely to the end of their days.

Snipp, snapp, snute
Her er eventyret ute!

Snip, snap, snout,
This tale's told out!

*From Asbjørnsen and Moe,
"Askeladden Som Kappåt med
Trollet." For another English
version see* Norwegian Folktales,
*translated by Iversen and Norman. This
is a classic troll story, clearly revealing
the dangerous nature of these forest
trolls and also showing how easily they
can be outwitted by a clever child.*

*Although adults sometimes feel
upset by the violence at the end of this
story, I have kept it, because it is so
satisfying, because children never seem
to be disturbed by it, and most of all
because I wouldn't dare change it —
Asbjørnsen and Moe would come to
haunt me if I did!*

SOME TROLLS DON'T CARRY THEIR HEARTS IN THEIR BODIES, BUT keep them carefully hidden. To defeat such a troll, you need all the help you can get, for it is too difficult to do alone. In this story it takes the cooperation of a really smart princess, a brave prince, and some good helpers to find the troll's heart.

The Troll with No Heart in His Body

ONCE UPON A TIME there was a king who had seven sons. The king loved his sons so much that when the time came for them to leave and look for brides, only the six eldest set off. The youngest prince remained at home for the king could not endure to be separated from all his sons at once. The other six promised to find a bride for their youngest brother as well.

They traveled far and wide until at last they came to a king who had six daughters, each more beautiful than the next. The brothers were so happy that they forgot all about their youngest brother and their promise. They were so much in love that they forgot their good sense and rode home using a shortcut over the mountains, past the castle of a mountain troll.

As soon as the troll heard the bridal party, he fell into a fit of fury.

"Who dares trespass on my land?" he roared and pointed his huge fingers at them. Immediately, the six princes with their six brides and the beautiful horses all turned to stone. It looked as though the troll had six stone statues in his courtyard.

The old king went nearly mad with grief waiting for his sons. Hugging the youngest, he said, "If it weren't for you I would have no reason to live."

"Oh, Father," said the youngest prince. "I too wish to go out into the world to seek my fortune. Who knows but that I may discover what has happened to my brothers as well."

The king was reluctant, but at last he gave in. He fitted the prince out as best

he could, but he had only a skinny old nag of a horse and a sack of food to give his son. With these provisions the prince rode off, waving to his old father.

After several days of riding he caught sight of a raven. This raven was so weak its wings dragged along the ground, and its feathers were dull and falling out.

"Please give me some food to eat," rasped the raven. "I haven't had a morsel for weeks. If you help me now, I will help you in your utmost need."

The prince looked at the raven. "I'm not so sure about the sort of help you can give me. But you are a sorry sight and I don't mind sharing my food with you."

As the raven ate, his wings grew sleek and strong. When he finished, he beat his wings, circled twice around the boy's head, and then flew off.

Next day the prince rode past a large salmon that flapped helplessly in the middle of the road. "Help me," gasped the salmon. "Please throw me into the river and I'll help you someday when you need it."

The prince shook his head a little and smiled. "I'd like to see what a salmon could do to help me! But you're surely not doing any good here in the middle of the road." He gently slipped the salmon into the river. The salmon swam up to the surface, gave a toss with his tail, and disappeared under the waves.

The prince rode on. The following day a wolf stood in the road. This wolf was so starved his ribs pierced through his skin and you could hear the wind whistling through his stomach. His fur hung in bits around him and he could scarcely keep his head above the ground.

"Give me your horse to eat," begged the wolf. "I haven't had a meal for two years. If you help me now, I will help you in your utmost need."

"No!" said the prince. "That's too much. I gave my food to a starving raven, I helped a salmon back into the river, but if I give you my horse to eat, how am I to travel?"

"Ride me! I will do whatever you ask, take you wherever you need to go. Just please, let me have your horse." Well, the wolf begged so long and so hard that the prince felt sorry for him and finally agreed.

While the wolf ate, his stomach filled in and his fur grew sleek and shiny. When he finished he lifted his head and looked at the boy with glittering green eyes. "Take the bit and the saddle and put them on me. You'll not be sorry for your kindness." Then the prince did as he was told, mounted the wolf, and away they flew as though the wind itself were taking them.

"Now tell me your errand," said the wolf. The prince told him about his brothers and his grieving father, and the wolf said, "Hang on, for I know just where to go." And they flew faster than the wind and in no time arrived at the troll castle.

"There stand your brothers and their brides," said the wolf nodding at the statues. When the prince recognized his brothers, terror gripped his heart.

"I might as well go home," said the prince. "How can I fight an enemy that can turn me into stone?"

"Don't give up! The troll who lives here is out hunting for the day, so you are safe now. Go inside. There you will met a princess whom the troll has stolen. She will tell you what to do."

When the princess saw the prince entering the castle, she called out, "What are you doing here? It is sure to be your death. The troll who lives here is due to

come back soon."

"I've come here to kill the troll and free my brothers who are standing out there turned to stone, and I will free you as well."

"Don't you know?" asked the princess. "*Nobody* can kill this troll, for he does not carry his heart in his body."

"Since I've come all this way, I might as well try my strength," insisted the prince.

When the princess saw she could not make him leave she said, "Well, since you will not leave, we must try to do the best we can. Creep under the bed over there and listen well to what he says when I speak with him, and be sure to lie there as quietly as you can."

The prince crept under the bed, and soon the mountain troll came thundering home. As he filled the huge doorway, his nose shot up and sniffed the air. "I smell the smell of human blood," he roared.

"Yes, yes," said the princess. "A magpie flew by this morning and dropped a human bone down the chimney. I threw it out and swept the castle, but the smell lingers." That calmed the troll, and he sat down for supper. As they sat there the princess sighed and said, "There's one thing I want so very much to know, if only I dared ask."

"Well, what can that be?" asked the troll.

"I should so like to know where your heart is, since you don't carry it about you."

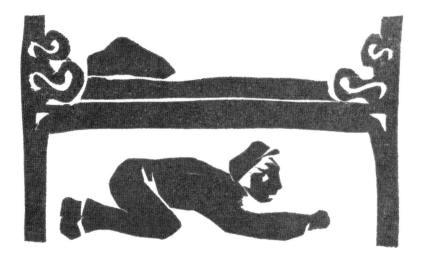

"Oh, that is one thing you needn't know anything about," said the troll, "but since you've asked, I keep it under the stone slab in front of the door."

"Aha, we shall soon see if we can't find that," thought the prince.

Next morning, as soon as the troll had left for the woods, the prince and the princess began to look for the heart under the stone slab, but they could not find it. "He has made a fool of me this time," said the princess, "but I will try again." She went out into the fields and collected all the prettiest flowers she could find and strewed them over the stone slab, which they had put back in its right place.

When the time came for the troll to return, the prince hid under the bed. Again the troll sniffed the air and complained about the human scent, but again the princess told him it was just the smell of a human bone dropped by a magpie. Then he noticed the flowers and wanted to know who had strewed them all over.

"Why, that was me, of course," said the princess.

"And why would you do a thing like that?" asked the troll.

"Well, you know how fond I am of you," said the princess. "When I knew you kept your heart there I just had to do it."

"OH HO HO," laughed the troll. "How could you believe I would keep my heart in a silly place like that?"

"How could I not believe, when you told me so yourself?" said the princess. "Where do you keep it then?"

"If you must know, it's over in the cupboard on the wall there," said the troll.

"Ah ha!" thought both the prince and the princess. "We will soon find it."

But the next morning, exactly the same thing happened. No matter how many cupboards they searched, they could not find the heart. "We must try once more," said the princess, and this time she hung garlands of flowers all over the cupboards. When the evening came the prince hid, and again the troll complained about the human smell. After the princess had calmed him, he noticed the garlands.

"What's the meaning of all this foolery?" bellowed the troll.

"Well, you know how fond I am of you. When you told me your heart is there I couldn't help doing it."

"How can you be so foolish and believe it?" asked the troll.

"How can I not believe it when you told me so yourself?" responded the princess. "I should very much like to know where it really is."

The troll could refuse her no longer and said, "Far, far away is a lake. On this lake stands a church, in this church there is a well, inside that well swims a duck, and inside that duck is an egg. Inside that egg, you'll find my heart. But it will do you no good to know this, for you will never go there."

"We'll see about that," said the prince to himself under the bed.

Early next morning the troll set out for the woods again. "Well, I suppose I might as well set off too," said the prince. Then he blushed and looked at the princess. "If I succeed and get rid of the troll would you be my bride?" he asked. The princess nodded and blushed too.

Outside, the wolf was waiting. "Jump on my back. I will find the way," he said when he heard what the troll had said.

Away they went, over mountains and fields and valleys until at last they came to the lake. The prince could not swim, but the wolf asked him not to be afraid. Then he plunged into the water with the prince on his back and swam to the island.

They walked ashore, and there in the middle of the island stood a church, just as the troll had said. But the church door was locked and the key hung high, high up on the steeple. The prince could see no way to climb up, but the wolf reminded him, "Now you must call the raven." And so he did! Immediately, the raven came, circled the steeple two times, took the key in his beak, and handed it to the prince.

In the center of the church was a large well, and in that well swam a duck. The prince called the duck until at last he lured her to him. Just as he caught the duck and lifted her out of the water, the duck let go of the egg and it dropped into the well.

Again, the prince did not know what to do, but the wolf reminded him, "You must call the salmon." He did, and the salmon came swimming through an underground river, and fetched the egg from the bottom of the well.

"Go outside and squeeze the egg," said the wolf. As soon as the prince squeezed the egg he could hear the troll roaring and screaming. "Squeeze it once more," said the wolf. This time the troll screamed even more piteously and begged

for his life. He would do all the prince wished, he said, if only he wouldn't squeeze his heart to bits.

"Tell him you will spare him only if he brings to life your six brothers, their brides, and their horses that he turned to stone," said the wolf.

The prince shouted the instructions. When the troll had restored the brothers, their brides, and their horses, the wolf said, "Now squeeze the egg to pieces." The prince took the egg between his two hands, lifted it high above his head, and squeezed it flat. Then they heard a tremendous explosion as the troll burst into thousands of pieces of rock.

The prince rode back on his friend the wolf, and when they got to the troll's castle, his six brothers and their brides stood there alive. The prince went inside the castle, fetched his own bride, and together they all rode home to the old king and the royal palace.

The king was so pleased and happy to see all his sons and their brides that he set about the wedding preparations at once. On the wedding day they had a grand feast. The king declared that never had he seen such lovely young people, but the loveliest of them all were the youngest prince and his bride. They should sit at the head of the table, the king said, for without their cleverness, none of them would be there.

Snipp, snapp, snute
Her er eventyret ute!

Snip, snap, snout,
This tale's told out!

From Asbjørnsen and Moe, "Risen Som Ikke Hadde Noe Hjerte på seg." *This story so captivated me as a child that I can still remember the first time my father read it to me. I find it has the same power with American children. A heartless and nasty troll, high adventure, magic, a really smart princess, a persevering prince, and a seemingly insurmountable problem—this story has it all. My telling is close to the Norwegian. A story as good as this one does not need many changes.*

Bibliography

Asbjørnsen, Peter Christian, and Jørgen Moe. *Norwegian Folktales*. Translated by Pat Shaw Iversen and Carl Norman. Oslo: Dreyers Forlag, 1960.

Asbjørnsen, Peter Christian, and Jørgen Moe. *Samlede Eventyr*. Oslo: Gyldendal Norsk Forlag, 1978.

Bettleheim, Bruno. *The Uses of Enchantment*. New York: Vintage Books, 1977.

Bø, Olav. *Trollmakter og Godvette. Overnaturlige Vesen i Norsk Folketru*. Oslo: Det Norske Samlaget, 1987.

Booss, Claire, editor. *Scandinavian Folk and Fairytales*. New York: Avenel Books, 1984.

Branston, Brian. *Gods of the North*. New York and London: Thames and Hudson, 1980.

Christiansen, Reidar Th. *Folktales of Norway*. Chicago: University of Chicago Press, 1964.

Dasent, George W. *Popular Tales from the Norse*. Edinburgh: Edmanston and Douglas, 1859.

D'Aulaire, Ingri, and Edgar Parin. *D'Aulaire's Trolls*. New York: Dell Publishing, 1972.

Haviland, Virginia. *Favorite Fairy Tales Told in Norway*. New York: Little, Brown, 1996.

Holbek, Bengt, and Iørn Piø. *Fabeldyr og Sagnfolk*. Copenhagen: Politikens Forlag, 1979.

Ingulstad, Frid, and Svein Solem. *Troll. Det Norske trollets Forskrekkelige Liv og Historie*. Oslo: Gyldendal Norsk Forlag, 1993.

Jones, Gwyn. *Scandinavian Legends and Folktales*. Oxford: Oxford University Press, 1956.

Klintberg, Bengt af. *Svenska Folksägner*. Stockholm: Bokforlaget Pan, 1977.

Kvideland, Reimund, and Henning K. Sehmsdorf. *Scandinavian Folk Belief and Legend*. Minneapolis: University of Minnesota Press, 1988.

Roll-Hansen, Joan, editor and translator. *A Time for Trolls*. Oslo: Nor-Media, 1962.

Simpson, Jacqueline, editor and translator. *Scandinavian Folktales*. London: Penguin, 1988.

Valebrokk, Eva. *Trollpakk og Andre Vetter*. Oslo: Boksenteret, 1995.

Sources

The folktales in this book are mainly from Peter Christian Asbjørnsen and Jørgen Moe's collection of Norwegian folktales titled *Samlede Eventyr*. From their first publication in 1841, these folktales gained enormous popularity, in part because their appearance coincided with a growing sense of national identity. Norway had achieved independence from Denmark in 1814 after four hundred years as a Danish colony. During this colonial period the official language of Norway had been closely modeled on Danish. Books were printed in Danish, and all higher education was conducted in Danish, causing, in a sense, the language and culture of Norway to go underground.

After independence Norwegians struggled to develop their own distinct identity, and the publication of the folktales became an important fuel for this national revival. The tales, which Asbjørnsen and Moe collected by traveling around the country, were felt to mirror the unique Norwegian landscape, with its towering mountains, craggy fjords, and deep forests. The eerie light, from endless daylight during midsummer to complete darkness during winter, is reflected in the clear contrast between good and evil, human and troll. The homespun sense of humor and the outspoken directness of the characters, from the peasant king down to the lowly Ashlad, revealed a stoic, no-nonsense approach to life felt to be typically Norwegian. In addition, the tales were recorded in the speech of the common folk, not in Danish. As such, these stories were the first works of literature published in Norwegian rather than in Danish.

Asbjørnsen and Moe's folktale collection became almost immediately a national classic. So important are these stories that whenever an official change

occurs in the Norwegian language, the first three books to be updated are the Bible, *The Official Book of Hymns,* and *Asbjørnsen and Moe's Collected Folktales.*

These are stories I have known since childhood. They were so important in my family that when I went off on my first day of elementary school, my father handed me a beautiful antique edition of the folktales as moral support. I received another lovely edition, this time in English, when I married my American "prince." It carries the following admonition: "To Lise with all good wishes and the hope that even though she may forget her Norwegian, she will never forget her Norwegian trolls." Well, I obviously never did. Within a year of beginning my life in America, I was telling troll stories, and I have never stopped since.

Like most Norwegians, I treasure the troll stories. Many of the tales in this collection have been part of my repertoire for more than twenty years. Most of them are close to the original Norwegian, but some changes have crept into the telling over the years. Since American children are not raised on trolls the way Norwegian children are, I have included more troll information. I do this both in the story itself as well as in my introduction to each story, just as I do in storytelling sessions.

In telling these tales orally I rely a great deal on my voice to show the character of the troll. To capture some of that in the writing, I have had to tell the stories out loud to myself as I type. This way I can tell when I whisper, when I roar, when I slow down, and when I speed up. All this I have tried to capture by choosing my verbs carefully, by using fewer and shorter words when I speak fast, or more words when I slow down. Throughout I have tried to keep the retellings simple and spare to clearly reveal the "good bones" of each story. This allows the powerful images

to stand out, and leaves plenty of room for the child's imagination to leap in.

Although there is some violence in these stories, I have resisted sanitizing them. Violence is an integral part of the stories. To remove it, is to remove the very threat the trolls pose and therefore the very real power that these stories have. Furthermore, my experience in the storytelling has shown me that children are far less disturbed by the violence than adults are, and that, as psychologist Bruno Bettleheim has pointed out, children need this kind of imaginary outlet for feelings they may have themselves.

The Norwegian folktales were first translated into English by Sir George W. Dasent. His translations are an excellent English language source of the folktales. The reader can assume that all the stories from Asbjørnsen and Moe are found in Dasent's *Popular Tales From the Norse,* Edinburgh, 1859.

J UST TO HELP YOU REMEMBER WHAT SLOW
thinkers trolls are, here's one last little story.

Trolls Shouting

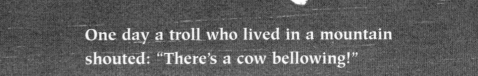

One day a troll who lived in a mountain
shouted: "There's a cow bellowing!"

Seven years later . . .

the troll who lived across the valley
answered: "Couldn't it just as well be a bull
as a cow?"

Another seven years passed . . .

before the troll in a third mountain, nearby, screamed, "If you two don't keep quiet and stop this commotion, I'll have to move!"

A Note from the Illustrator

MY GRANDFATHER, GUSTAV OLSEN, CAME TO CHICAGO FROM NORWAY in 1907, just before my father was born. When I was a girl I liked the meals my dad cooked of thin pancakes with lingonberries, a recipe from faraway Norway. In recent years I started to wonder what the stories of my own ethnic heritage were, other than Mickey Mouse, *Alice in Wonderland, The Secret Garden,* and *The Wind in the Willows.*

As I have lived on the land in northern Minnesota for thirty years, I have come to identify with the stories of the native people here and the way they tell the heartbeat and character of the land. Now I have discovered the troll stories, in which the rocks and rumblings have explanations in a similar way.

I visited Norway in 1993, and my thoughts of picturing the trolls in a book began. The west coast of Norway feels a lot like the north shore of Lake Superior, where I live now. This area was settled by Norwegian fishermen. The ones I know have the same sense of humor as the trolls in "The Handshake"; they help you out, but not without a joke or two to tease you.

The art for this book was done by making woodblock prints, carving the design into a flat block of wood, rolling colored ink onto the surface, and then printing onto paper. My son Jeremy Bowen applied his competent hand collaborating on the printing. I have used the great heritage of Norwegian woodcarving and design, particularly from the very old stave churches, in bordering the pictures. I have loved getting to know and respect the art of Theodor Kittelsen, the Norwegian illustrator who actually drew the trolls from life in the early 1900s.